Look What I See!
Where Can I Be?
At the Synagogue

by Dia L. Michels

Photographs by
Michael J.N. Bowles

5764/2003
Platypus Media, LLC
Washington, DC

For my grandparents
Gwen & Bill
Rose & Abe
for keeping our heritage alive

Enjoy these other *Look What I See!* books by Dia L. Michels
In the Neighborhood
At Home
With My Animal Friends
Visiting China

Activity Guide available at PlatypusMedia.com

Library of Congress Cataloguing-in-Publication Data

Michels, Dia L.
  At the synagogue / by Dia L. Michels ; photographs by Michael J.N. Bowles.
    p. cm. —(Look what I see! Where can I be? ; 5)
  Summary: By viewing a detail from a photograph that is revealed on the following
page, the reader is invited to guess in what part of a synagogue a baby wakes up.
  ISBN 1-930775-16-4 (alk. paper)
  1.   Synagogues—Juvenile literature. 2. Judaism—Customs and practices—Juvenile
literature. 3. Fasts and feasts—Judaism—Juvenile literature. [1. Synagogues. 2.
Judaism—Customs and practices.] I. Bowles, Michael J. N., ill. II. Title.
  BM653.M532002   2002022363
  296.4—dc21

Platypus Media is committed to the promotion and protection of breastfeeding.
We donate six percent of our profits to breastfeeding organizations.
Platypus Media, LLC
627 A Street, NE
Washington, DC 20002
PlatypusMedia.com

1 2 3 4 5 6 7 8 9

Series editor: Ellen E.M. Roberts, Where Books Begin, New York, NY
Project editor: Rachel Connelly, Ph.D., Brunswick, ME
Project consultants: Naomi Bromberg Bar-Yam, Ph.D., Newton, MA
Gretchen Hesbacher, Washington, DC
Project management: Maureen Graney, Washington, DC
Book design: Douglas Wink, Inkway Graphics, Santa Fe, NM
Production consultant: Kathy Rosenbloom, New York, NY

Special thanks to the staff and members of Temple Beth El Hebrew, Alexandria, VA, for their welcoming support of our family.
The author would also like to thank the Deutsch family for sharing their home with us
and Washington Hebrew Congregation, Washington, DC, for the use of their facilities.

Manufactured in the United States of America.

It is fun to go
to the synagogue
with my family.

On Sunday,
I fell asleep
in my stroller.

When I woke up,
I saw a *Kiddush* cup.

Where was I?

By the *chuppah* at a wedding.

On Monday,
I fell asleep
in a classroom.

When I woke up,
I saw a *shofar*.

Where was I?

In class
learning about
Rosh Hashanah.

On Tuesday,
I fell asleep
in my bike seat.

When I woke up,
I saw a *lulav* and *etrog*.

Where was I?

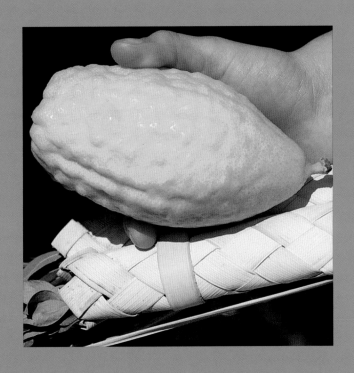

Rejoicing in the *sukkah*.

On Wednesday,
I fell asleep
in my basket.

When I woke up,
I saw the *Torah*.

Where was I?

In the social hall celebrating *Simchat Torah.*

On Thursday,
I fell asleep
in the backpack.

When I woke up,
I saw a *chai*.

Where was I?

Singing with
the cantor at
Hebrew school.

On Friday,
I fell asleep
in my Daddy's arms.

When I woke up,
I saw a *menorah*.

Where was I?

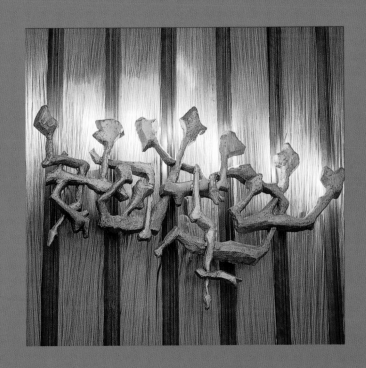

In the sanctuary for *Shabbat* services.

On Saturday,
I fell asleep
in my Mommy's lap.

When I woke up,
I saw a braided candle.

Where was I?

At our *Havdalah* ceremony.

I always like
going to the synagogue
with my family.

About Jewish Life

Jewish weddings are filled with symbols of joy and hope for the future. The bride and groom drink sweet fruit of the vine—wine or grape juice—from the same *Kiddush cup* to symbolize the happiness of their union. The bride and groom stand under a *chuppah*, or canopy, that represents the home they will make together. Jewish weddings are occasions for singing, dancing and joyous celebration with family and friends.

Rosh Hashanah, often seen as the Jewish New Year, occurs in early autumn at the end of the harvest season. It is celebrated with the blowing of the *shofar,* a ram's horn that produces a trumpet-like sound. On *Rosh Hashanah,* Jews celebrate the start of a sweet new year by eating apples or *challah* (a braided sweet bread that is served on *Shabbat* and holidays) dipped in honey. Some Jews eat pomegranates with the hope of having plenty of health and happiness in the New Year—with good things as numerous as the seeds of the fruit.

Sukkot, a week-long holiday, occurs two weeks after *Rosh Hashanah*. The fall harvest festival, *Sukkot* is the "Festival of Booths," named after the temporary hut, or *sukkah,* in which Jewish farmers lived during the harvest time. To celebrate the holiday, some Jewish families build a *sukkah* in which they eat and, weather permitting, sleep during this festival week. During *Sukkot,* the *lulav* (made of a palm, myrtle and willow branch bound together in a braided holder) and *etrog* (citron fruit) are shaken in all directions as a reminder that God is everywhere.

Simchat Torah is a joyous holiday that comes near the end of *Sukkot*. It means "rejoicing for the *Torah*" and celebrates the beginning of the reading cycle of the *Torah* (the first five books of the Hebrew Bible). Each week in the synagogue, Jews read a portion of the *Torah* scroll. At the end of the year, the scroll must be rewound so it can be read from the beginning again. On *Simchat Torah*, the last portion of the *Torah* is read, the scroll is rewound, and the first portion is begun in an ongoing cycle. The festive celebration includes parading around the synagogue and singing and dancing with the scroll.

Many people are familiar with the phrase *"L'chayim!"* which means "To life!" **Chai,** the root of the word, is the Hebrew word for "life." *Chai* is often used as a design on jewelry and other ornaments. In Hebrew, each letter of the alphabet has a numerical equivalent. The word *chai* adds up to 18—making it a special number for Jews. Charitable contributions are often given in multiples of $18.

A **menorah** is a candelabrum. Many people are familiar with the nine-branched menorah used on the holiday of *Chanukah*. The *Chanukah* menorah, called a *chanukiah*, holds a candle for each of the eight nights of the holiday along with a *shamash*, or helper candle. The seven-branched menorah is symbolic of those found in the ancient Temple in Jerusalem and some say it symbolizes God's creation of the world in seven days.

Havdalah, which means "separation," is a brief service at the end of the Sabbath day. The Sabbath day, or *Shabbat*, is the Jewish day of rest, which starts at sundown Friday evening and concludes at sundown on Saturday. *Shabbat* begins with a ceremony that includes candle-lighting and blessings over children, wine and bread. The blessings acknowledge God's role as creator of all. Shabbat ends with the *Havdalah* ceremony, which includes lighting, and then extinguishing, a braided candle and blessings over wine and sweet spices. These symbols stimulate all the senses to say goodbye to the *Sabbath* and welcome the new week. *Havdalah* helps us bridge from the holy *Shabbat* to the rest of the week to come.

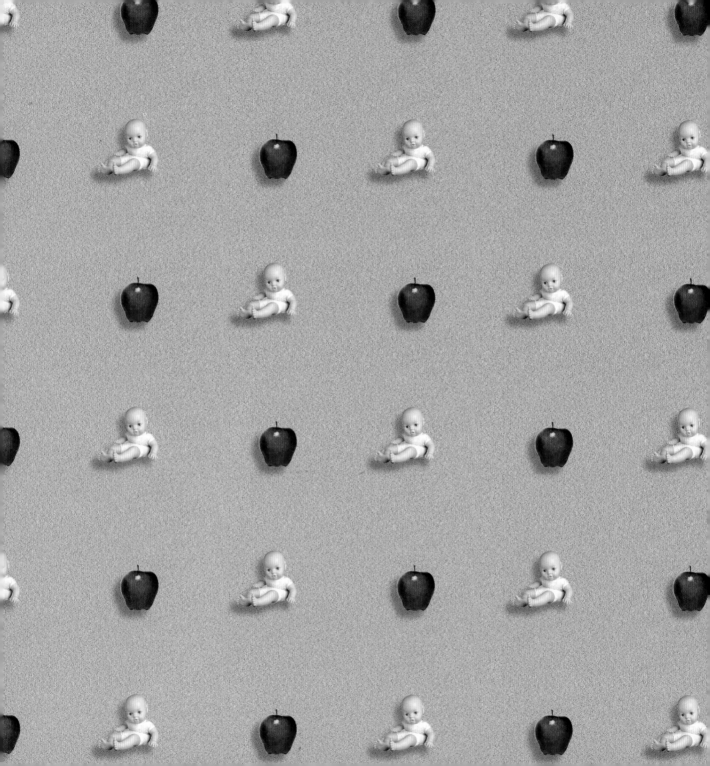